ride their bikes

Jean and Gareth Adamson

Blackie Children's Books

BLACKIE CHILDREN'S BOOKS

Published by the Penguin Group
Penguin Books Ltd, 27 Wrights Lane, London W8 5TZ, England
Penguin Books USA Inc., 375 Hudson Street, New York, NY 10014, USA
Penguin Books Australia Ltd, Ringwood, Victoria, Australia
Penguin Books Canada Ltd, 10 Alcorn Avenue, Toronto, Ontario, Canada M4V 3B2
Penguin Books (NZ) Ltd, 182-190 Wairau Road, Auckland 10, New Zealand

Penguin Books Ltd, Registered Offices: Harmondsworth, Middlesex, England

First published 1992 by Blackie Children's Books
7 9 10 8 6

Copyright © 1992 Jean and Gareth Adamson

The moral right of the author and illustrator has been asserted

Made and printed in Great Britain by William Clowes Limited, Beccles and London

A CIP catalogue record for this book is available from the British Library

ISBN   0 216 93135 5 Hbk
ISBN   0 216 93134 7 Pbk

When Topsy and Tim came downstairs
on the first morning of the
summer holidays, they saw two
gleaming bikes standing in
the kitchen.

'Are they really for us?' asked Topsy.
'Yes,' said Dad. 'We can't go away
on holiday this summer, so you will
have lots of time to learn to ride them.'
Topsy tried to climb on to her bike,
but the saddle was too high. Her
feet didn't reach the ground.

'Oh, dear,' said Tim, 'Topsy's bike
is too big for her.'
Mummy found a spanner and lowered
Topsy's saddle. Now her toes could
touch the ground safely. Mummy checked
Tim's bike too.

The new bikes had stabilizer wheels on them, so Topsy and Tim were able to ride them round the garden.

Jinder watched them over the fence.
'I like your new bikes,' she said.
'Can you ride them without stabilizers?'
'Not yet,' said Tim, 'but we're
going to learn.'

That afternoon, Topsy and Tim asked
Mummy if they could take their
stabilizers off.
'All right,' said Mummy.
She took them off with the spanner.
'Now see how far you can ride,'
she said.

'Easy peasy,' said Topsy.
But it wasn't. Learning how to
balance was quite difficult.
Topsy and Tim kept falling off.
'I can see you're going to need
the helmets I bought,' said Mummy.

The next day, Mummy took Topsy
and Tim to the park.
'There's plenty of space here and
no dangerous traffic,' she said.

Topsy and Tim saw some children riding BMX bikes and doing clever stunts. One of them shouted, 'Hallo, Topsy and Tim. I like your new bikes.' It was Josie Miller.

'I'm going to do stunts on my bike,' said Topsy.
'I'm going to do wheelies and bunny hops,' said Tim.
'You'll have to learn to ride your bikes first,' said Mummy.

'I'm ready,' said Tim. He got on
his bike. Mummy held on to his
saddle and pushed him along.

'Pedal, Tim,' she said. After a few
steps she let go of the saddle.
Wobble, wobble, wobble, went Tim.
'Keep going,' puffed Mummy.
Tim kept going...faster and faster.
'Use your brake to slow down,'
called Mummy.

Tim tried to use his brake but
he lost his balance and fell off.
Luckily he was wearing his helmet,
so he wasn't hurt.

'My turn,' called Topsy.
Mummy started Topsy off. Then she
let go.
'Ooo-er,' went Topsy. 'Don't let go!'
'You're doing fine,' said Mummy.
'Keep it up!'

Topsy and Tim kept practising.
At last Topsy could start by
herself and Tim could stop
without falling off.

'Well done,' said Mummy. 'I think
it's time for a rest. Let's go
home and have something to eat.'

They rode back through the park.

When they reached the park gates,
Mummy told them to get off their
bikes and push them along the
pavement. 'It's dangerous for you
to ride your bikes near a road,'
she said.

They were nearly home when a voice
called, 'Hallo, twins.' It was
Louise Lewis's big sister, Carol, on
her bike. Carol was wearing a helmet
and a brightly coloured band.

'What's that band for?' asked Topsy.
'It's a safety sash,' explained Carol,
'so that car drivers can see me easily.'
'Should we wear safety sashes?' asked
Topsy.
'Not yet,' said Carol. 'You are too
young to ride on the road.'

'Carol had to pass her Cycling
Proficiency Test at school before
she was allowed to ride on the road,'
said Mummy.

'Guess what, Dad,' said Tim that evening. 'We've learned to ride our bikes!'